Patricia Lee Gauch, Editor

PHILOMEL BOOKS A division of Penguin Young Readers Group.   Published by The Penguin Group.   Penguin Group (USA) Inc., 375 Hudson Street, New York, NY 10014, U.S.A.   Penguin Group (Canada), 90 Eglinton Avenue East, Suite 700, Toronto, Ontario M4P 2Y3, Canada (a division of Pearson Penguin Canada Inc.). Penguin Books Ltd, 80 Strand, London WC2R 0RL, England.   Penguin Ireland, 25 St. Stephen's Green, Dublin 2, Ireland (a division of Penguin Books Ltd). Penguin Group (Australia), 250 Camberwell Road, Camberwell, Victoria 3124, Australia (a division of Pearson Australia Group Pty Ltd).   Penguin Books India Pvt Ltd, 11 Community Centre, Panchsheel Park, New Delhi - 110 017, India.   Penguin Group (NZ), 67 Apollo Drive, Rosedale, North Shore 0632, New Zealand (a division of Pearson New Zealand Ltd).   Penguin Books (South Africa) (Pty) Ltd, 24 Sturdee Avenue, Rosebank, Johannesburg 2196, South Africa. Penguin Books Ltd, Registered Offices: 80 Strand, London WC2R 0RL, England.

Published simultaneously in Canada.   Manufactured in China by South China Printing Co. Ltd.

Design by Semadar Megged.   Text set in 20-point Stellar Delta.   The art was done in watercolor.
Library of Congress Cataloging-in-Publication Data
Ichikawa, Satomi.   My little train / Satomi Ichikawa.   p. cm.
Summary: A little train goes for a ride, taking all the stuffed animals where they want to go.
[1. Railroad trains—Fiction. 2. Animals—Fiction. 3. Toys—Fiction.] I. Title.
PZ7.I16Mv 2010   [E]—dc22   2009044772
ISBN 978-0-399-25453-6
2 4 6 8 10 9 7 5 3 1

MY LITTLE
TRAIN

Satomi Ichikawa

PHILOMEL BOOKS
An Imprint of Penguin Group (USA) Inc.

My little train goes chug
chug chug, chugging
into Central Station.
Whoo whoo whooo!
See all the passengers who want
to come aboard?

"Where do you want to go?
I will take you anywhere,"
says the train.
Whoo whoo whooo.
"To the pond," says a duck. Quack, quack.
"To the field," says a sheep. Baa, baa.
"To the forest," says a monkey. Ki, ki.
"To the mountain," says a bear. Grr, grr.

"Here we go!" says the train.
Whoo whoo!
Across the hill, chug chug,
over the bridge, whoo whoo,
through the tunnel, chug chug, whoo whoo.
Quack quack,
Baa baa,
Grr grr,
Ki ki ki,
say all the happy passengers.

"First stop! The pond,
the pond,"
says the train.

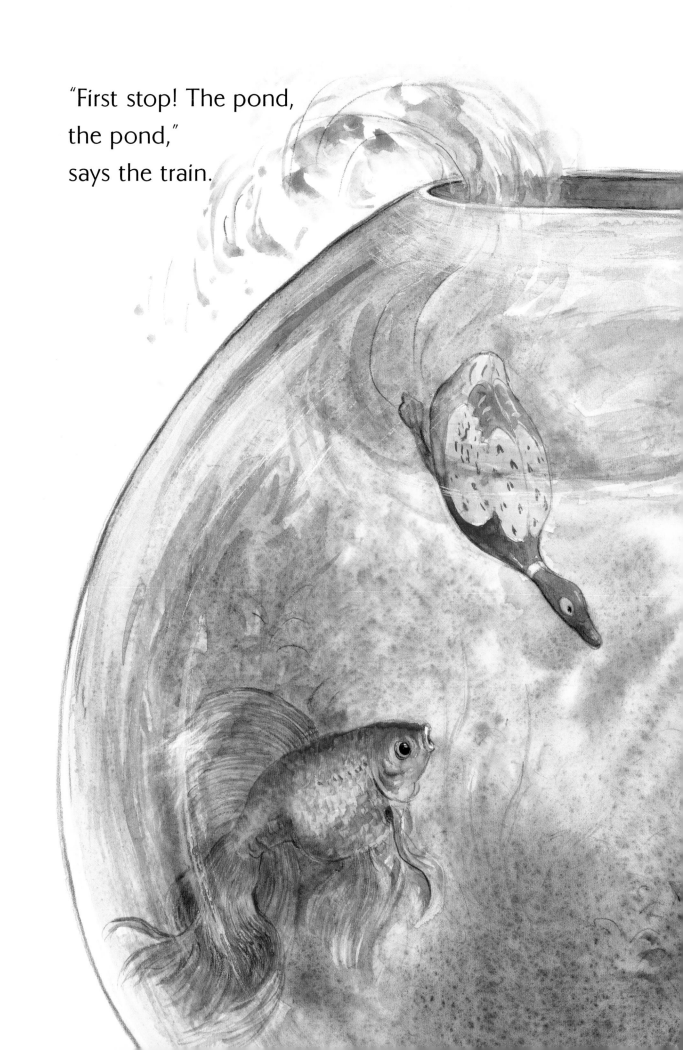

The duck jumps out and dives
into the pond.
"Good-bye, Duck!" says the
train, whoo whoo.

"Next stop! The field, the field," says the train.
The sheep jumps out and runs into the poppy field.
"Have a nice day, Sheep!" says the train, whoo whoo.

"Next stop! The forest, the forest,"
says the train.
The monkey hops out and swings
into the branches.
"See you next time," says the
train, whoo whoo.

Here comes the mountain! The mountain!
Huff a puff, huff a puff, sighs the train.
"Last stop, the mountaintop."

"Don't forget your lunch box," says the train,
and the bear climbs out.
"Be careful," says the train, whoo whoo.
Everyone has gone now. Good job, good job.

"Bravo, Train," says a little voice.

It's a little kangaroo. Where did he come from?

"I love trains," says the little kangaroo.

"Glad to hear it. Where do you want to go?"

says the train, whoo whoo.

"For a ride, a ride!" says the little kangaroo,
and they go
across the mountains, chug chug,

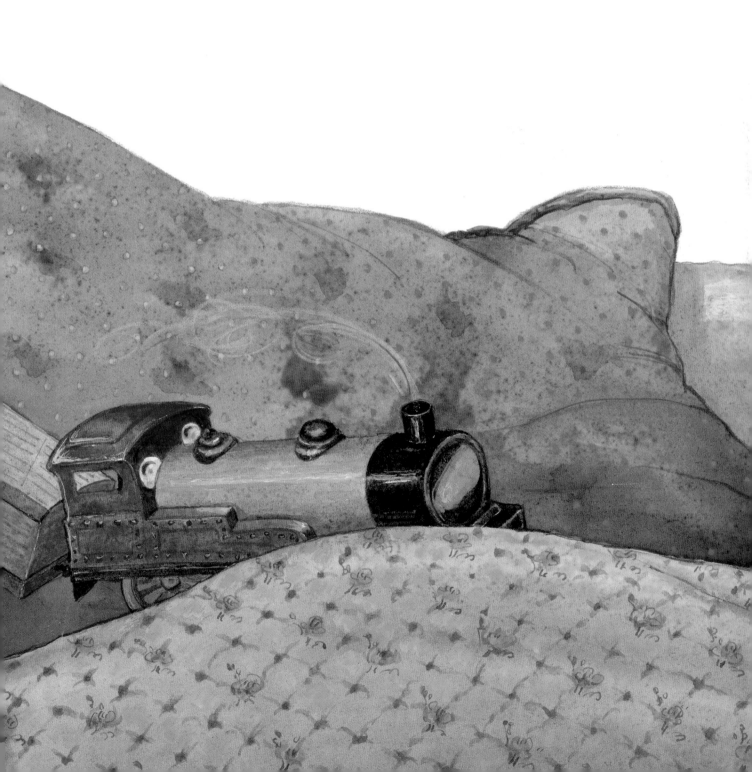

over the bridge, whoo whoo,
through the tunnel, chug chug, whoo whoo.
"This is fun," says the little kangaroo.

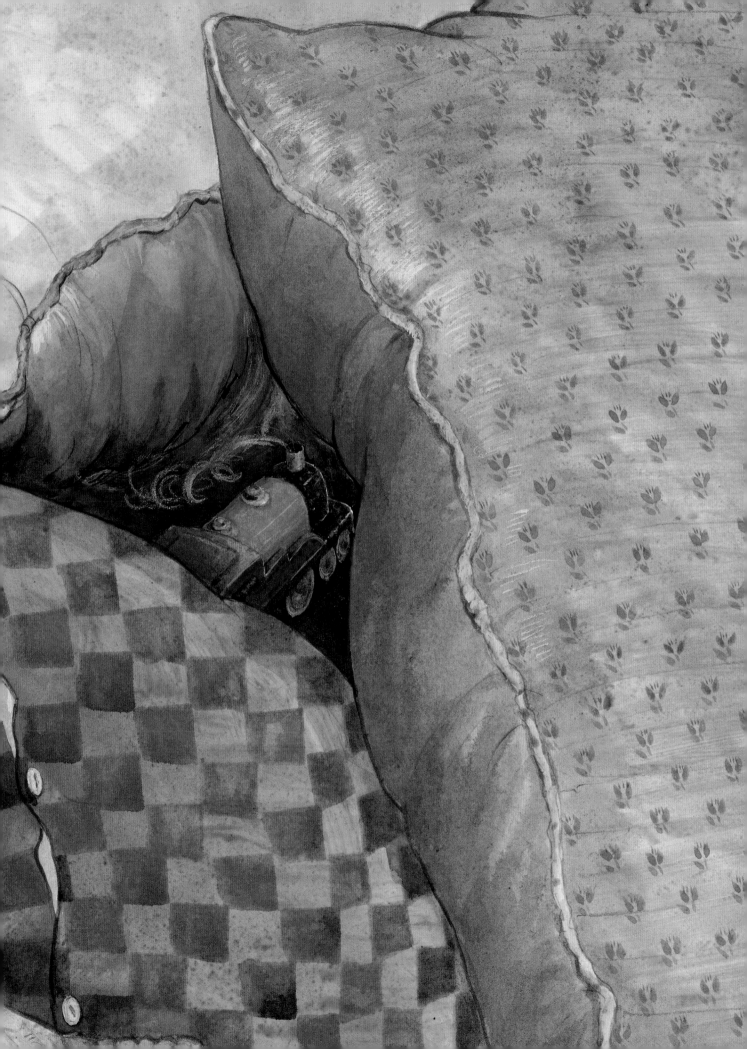

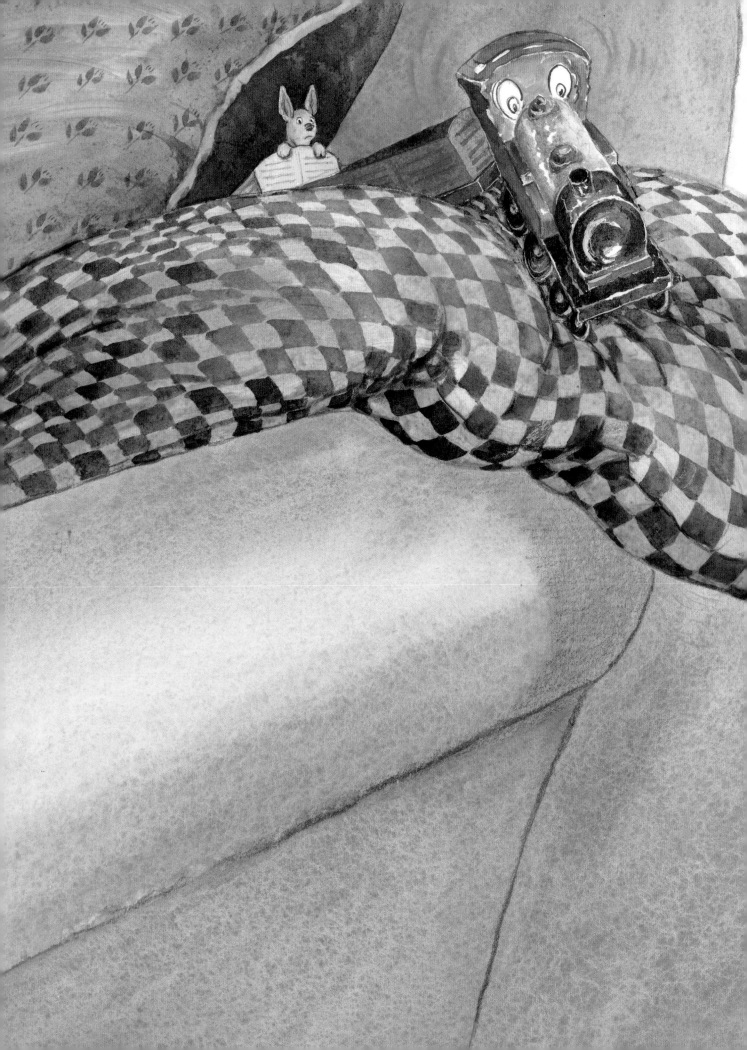

Then they reach a cliff!
Whoo whooo whoooooooooo!
"Hold on tight, Little Kangaroo!"

The train falls down,
bump, bump, bump . . .
and stops.

The little kangaroo hops out,
hop, hop, hop,
and pushes the train.
Huff a puff, huff a puff.
Up goes one car.
Up goes another car.
Up goes the engine.
"Hooray, Little Kangaroo!
Glad you were with me."

"Now, where do you want to go?"
says the train, whoo whoo.
"To my pocket! To my pocket!"
says the little kangaroo.
"Where did you leave it?"
asks the train, chug chug.

"At Central Station!"
says the little kangaroo.
"Ahhhhhhhhhhhhhhh. Okay then.
Central Station, here we come,"
says the train, chug chug, whoo whoo.

Here is Central Station.

See all the passengers waiting for the train?

See someone waiting for the kangaroo, too?

"It's Mama. It's Mama," shouts the little kangaroo,
and jumps into her pocket.

"Good-bye, Train, and thank you,"
says the little kangaroo.
"Come aboard anytime,
my little big friend,"
says the train, chug chug,
whoo whoo whoooo.